River of My Soul

River of My Soul

Victor Akinrinmade

ISBN: 978-1-64945-372-3   (Paperback Edition)
ISBN: 978-1-64945-373-0   (Hardcover Edition)
ISBN: 978-1-64945-377-8   (E-book Edition)

Book Ordering Information

Phone Number: 347-901-4929 or 347-901-4920
Email: info@globalsummithouse.com
Global Summit House
www.globalsummithouse.com

Printed in the United States of America

Contents

The She That Is Good For Me 1

Hold My Pen for You 2

I Don't Mind...3

Your Love..4

The Beauty Leading Me to Happiness...6

You Have To Know 7

I Love Her Much 8

She Loves Me True...9

How Many Times?...10

All Alone..11

Never Happened Before 12

The Morning Star 13

The Word through Love That Says 14

Life's Just a Drop of Water..15

Nature Talking to Me 16

She's Always My Home 17

Song of My Soul..18

Not Worrying for the Next 19

Can't Waste in Sand...20

The Day Will Come...22

Lead Me On, My Love..23

Strength Needs Love 24

For the Young at Heart...25

Love Alone I Want 26

For Love Alone..27

I Move On 28

So Think, My love 30

When Love Alone 31

I Can See Smiles 32

Give Me Your Love 33

Whisper to Me 35
Tell Me the Truth 36
A Stepping Stone 40
O', See the Tears 42
The Powerful, Happy Prince 43
Like a Flowing Stream 44
In Love I Put My Hope 46
The Battle Is Fought and Won 49
I Remember the Day 50
My Heart Love You 51
Don't Make Me Cry..52
What Brilliant Eyes You've Got 53
I Will Meet You 54
The Candle Burns..55
What Would I Say? 56
The Rhyming Talk...57
The Tunnel of Life 58
The Bottom of Hope...59
Your Lips but Drips...60
An Arrow Shot 61

The She That Is Good For Me

How scare is she,
How rare is she
who won my lonesome
heart.

She is but a crown,
she is but a bead,
she is but a dear
to plan my life.

The greatest man,
the wisest man
must have the she
that is good for him.

She's fair, I know,

and kind she is;

she is blessed by wisdom

herself.

The she that is good
for me will come out
of her lonesome shell
and show her face
to me.

Hold My Pen for You

She's the one I love,
I can't but hold my
pen for the one I
love so dear.

She never sends her
piece to me;
she never says her love.

The only piece I
got of her is an odd
sort of a thing.

She's the one I
love, I know;
The smoke is rising high,
but things will
turn out right.

I Don't Mind

Your breeze of love
Just blows to me,
And I know it is
true.

Going 'round the world,
as the world will say,
I know your love
draws mine
along.

Being patient,
being kind,
being honest with
self-control,
and a gentle heart
to crown it all
makes me yearn
for you.

I must say,
I don't mind loving
you.

Your Love

You have not met
her for sure;
you can't miss her,
my dear.

She is your other half,
she is for you,
she will change your
life for sure.

How could you
missed her, dear?

You've not vigilant
enough.

With her slight wave
and soft smile, dear,
she comes to you on
time.

How could you have
missed her love?

You must have doubted
her for sure.

It hurts her to the
marrow;
you must have wounded
her much.
Thinking of you

To think of you,
to talk of you,
I wonder where to stop.

Thinking of you brings
tears into my eyes;
how could I forget?

Like the rainbow so
sure, my dear,
So strong is the bond of
my love.

Man could not say,
words could not tell,
the misery behind
it all.

As the failing tears
just come on and on,
the love is as
strong as death,
my dear.

Thinking of you
brings tears into my
eyes.

The Beauty Leading Me to Happiness

It is the smile I
know;
It is the eyes I
saw;
it is the beauty in
her leading me
to happiness.

She is the talk of
the town;
she bends the way
I talk,
so shy and fair,
my dear,
oh dear, I love her
so much.

Her name is like a
golden thread;
she seems to me a
sunbeam;
the smile I've never
seen before;
I love no one but
you.

You Have To Know

Trusting the word to
say,
how it goes along with
me.

Like a flower so tender,
dear,
so sensitive am I;
I could cry when my
love refuses to
trust.

I will bring you honey,
I will bring your bread,
I will bring you goodies
all my days,
if you just trust
In me.

My love, you have to know
the key that turns my
heart.

I'm as light as a feather,
and I will make you
a loving one.

I Love Her Much

A good character is a
golden shine;
she told me once,
she told me twice
that I mustn't just
let her alone.

She is a crown of
wisdom, but very few
know her so.

She speaks so sweet
but
too damn low,
unless the drum is
low.

I love her much,
I want her much;
how I wish I could
be her love.

I want her once,
I want her twice,
I want her all to myself.

Don't think I cheat!
I know I don't.

She Loves Me True

My dear loves me;
she does love me;
she thinks and runs very
fast for me.

She cares for me,
she cares for me,
in winter,
in spring,
in summer.

She loves me real,
she loves me true,
she shows her face out
when I need her
most.

In my few years I still
want her . . .
her love to stick
as ever.

You think me wise,
you think me a fool,
but I know this:
I love her much.

How Many Times?

You feel so blue,
she feels so hurt,
and the children
suffer, too.

You forgot to show
your love;
you forgot to tell
your love.

Kissing,
holding,
and talking,
out of date

It hurts her so
when you jest at
her
in the presence of
friends and children.

Tell her your love,
show her your love,
and you will
know her love.

All Alone

I'm all alone in the
World.

All alone in a room,
with silence and unhappiness
as close companions.

All alone,
locked away
in a room with no
windows or doors.

I'm all alone in the
world,
as the laughter of
my life fades away.

All alone
as the sound
of my silence screams
to God!

But He heard the voice
of my cry,
'cause He knows I'm
all alone.

Never Happened Before

It shook the wall,
it shook the king,
it's never happened before.

He did what no man has
done;
he saw what no man has seen.

The king will have a
feast!

Call in the beauties;
call in the lovers;
bring Israel's vessels
and let them
drink!

Praise the iron,
praise the gold;
let us cheer for our
great king's feast.

But, like a light,
the colour changed;
a strange hand is writing
on the wall.

Your kingdom is come
to an end, o' king,
Weighted and found
wanting.

The Morning Star

Have a look at the
morning star;
have a look at the
day.

He said you come,
he said you go,
but the pride of life
sailed him to death.

The burning fleet,
the flying bird,
dumped on the land or
sea.

How strong the ship,
how weak it sails;
the proud and arrogant
all feel the same.

He was created fine
and good,
but his pride for life
blew him so high;
he wants to be
the highest!

The Word through Love That Says

The nightingale is singing
song, and life is but
made a smile.

Remember love,
remember love,
and so she held the key.

The key to life,
the key to joy,
the key to history
is made.

But how, o' man,
but how, o' maid,
you're wise, but fools
of one so made.

You're made so fine
with brains so good,
but fools regret her
love.

The nightingale . . .
the nightingale,
collect the love
man so disowns.

Man so disowns the
way to life,
and chooses death
instead.

Life's Just a Drop of Water

My life goes by,
my life goes by,
just like the morning
cloud, it just goes
by.

I think it so,
I think it so,
that it's just like
a drop of water.

Once,
once,
once it goes
it never comes back.

I cry for you,
I weep for you,
o' little Bob of my life.

I just wish it would take
some time
before my little life
just goes right
by.

Nature Talking to Me

The trees,
the mountains,
the rivers,
how they all talked to
me.

The said come,
they said see,
they said the master has
made a fountain of
water.

I looked all up,
I looked all down,
but what I saw
only set me
ablaze.

The sun,
the moon,
the stars,
all just smiled at
the folly of man.

I smiled it through,
I smiled it off,
but I hope
I'm not a
fool?

She's Always My Home

Once I was angry,
once I was gone,
once I was looking,
but she's always
my home.

Go through the waters,
go through the air,
go on the land;
I know she's
there.

Where can I go?

Where can I be?

Where can I dream
my home is?

Sweet home is there;
the joy is there,
the love is there;
I know she's
there.

Once I think,
once I look,
once I dream,
my home is there.

Song of My Soul

The song of my life is this,
I know:
to live life with joy
and smile.

But like a fool I roam
about;
the world is just too
wide.

I can't make it;
I can't pass through,
but one thing is clear:
he will sail me though.

The song of my soul is
this, o' man:
I need to
trust,
obey,
and life will be like my
dreams.

Not Worrying for the Next

The little bird woke early
in the morning;
looking at the sky,
it closes it eyes,
it stretches its legs,
it shakes its body and
begins to sing.

From the nest it flew to
the nearest stream, to suck
the coolest drink.

With God's blessing, it
flies away,
searching for its daily
meal.

Not worrying for the next,
but the night falls;
back at its brook
it thanks the Lord
with the best voice
it can make.

Sleeping soundly is the
little bird with terrible
storms around.

Can't Waste in Sand

The truth is bitter in truth;
so says a sage in
town.

O' man,
o' man, you see,
you see them throw their
stones
at the old and wearied
man
who only said the
truth.

The truth is bitter, I
know,
but how many say
it?

But look at the soul of
man that speaks the truth
always.

The Lord looks down
at him
and smiles
at him.

The best of his chariots
he sends to take his
soul up home.

His soul can't waste
in sand;
the Lord can't bear it
once.

The Lord is lonely for
him;
the Lord wants just
his kiss.

Tears never fall from
his eyes again;
he lives more and
more,
never to die again.

The Day Will Come

The master of the
game you are,
my love.

What makes you
the way
are?

All days I wonder
what to do,
but before I know,
love leads me
on.

O' love, I know
the day will
come,
just like a light
dawning in my
life.

I see you come
in through the
door,
and what I see,
I'm pleased with
it.

Lead Me On, My Love

A river that flows
in and out of
my soul.

The way to my
soul, I said.

Lead me on, my
love,
lead me on, my
joy,
as you lead me on
my own.

I refuse to let
you go, my
love.

How can you say go
when you mean
stay?

You call me
as I wait for
you.

Strength Needs Love

Help, my love,
I said to her;
help, my joy,
I said;
I need your shoulder to
lean on.

How can you
know?

How can you
say
that with arms so
strong
I will move my
legs?

Sometimes, my
love,
strength needs
love,
as love, you know,
is food for
strength.

O', my dear love,
I need
your shoulder to
lean on.

For the Young at Heart

In love I look at this
very sky,
as wonderful love engulfs
my day.

In my sky I see
you,
and love
will win the day.

O' come, my love,
the day is young;
as you can see,
we're still but
young.

For young at heart
is youth indeed;
for where love is
is youth, my love.

My love comes down
and meets your
love,
the love that loves
you all your
life.

Love Alone I Want

Why wonder so, my
love?

I've seen that love
is strong, my
love.

O' help me, love;
I say, my
dear,
what brings me home
today, my love?

Love, you know, is
strong, my
love,
and love alone I want, my
dear.

Please help me, dear,
my love,
my own,
for you alone
I want, my
love.

For Love Alone

Let it be, my
love,
let it be, I
say.

When hope is come
your way, my
love,
let it be, I
say.

Why should you keep
your hands behind
and wish it would go
away, my
love?

Let it be, I
say,
let it be, my
love,
for love alone will
break the yoke.

So let it be, my
love,
for love will stand
the test, my
dear,
and so do you, my
love.

I Move On

I've learnt to suffer,
my love, I
said,
to live with hope
and with none, my
love.

I've seen the wonder
of life, my
dear,
as I wonder about my life
my love.

How can I sink,
my dear?
For I'm created so
strong and good.

O' dear, my love,
I fight it through,
for love, you know,
will win the race.

I move on with
strength so great,
to make my love
yearn for me.

I stay in love with
You, my dear,
as love will wait
for me, my love.

Sometimes I wonder
where to go,
as life becomes so dull,
my dear.

O' stand and move, I
say to you;
I know that joy will
come at last.

Where hope is love,
patience will come,
and one must wait
for it, my love.

As you can see, my
Love, I say,
that I will stand
as my days go
by.

So Think, My love

Think before you
step, my love,
as you can see that
love flies.

So think before you
step, my love,
for like a part
without reverse
you are, my darling one.

How can you say
you start again?

The past is buried,
and you can't
touch it.

So think, my love, before
you step,
for a wrongful step will
ruin your life.

So wait for love,
stick up to her,
as love, you know, will
make your life.

When Love Alone

I've done the thing
I've got to do,
and a regret, dear,
I refused to
have.

How can you say I've
got to cry,
when for love alone
I've stood my
ground?

As you can see, my
Love, I say,
I stick to love for
you, my love.

Have no regret, my
love, I say,
for doing right
is no regret.

You smell nice, love;
you glow nice, love,
and I have no regrets
for you,
my love.

I Can See Smiles

Thanking my God,
I say to myself,
and waiting for my
time to come.

I've seen my pain
has gone, my
love,
when hope once gone
now lives again.

See it, my love:
I live again,
as time is but gone to
live again.

I can see smiles,
I can see joy,
since hope was dead
and lives again.

My love, I can only
tell you so,
for my hope is
come to stay.

Give Me Your Love

Help me do right,
I said to her;
I'm trying to, she
said to me.

I need your help;
I need yours too;
I guess we both need
love, I said.

How can you say walk
through it, my
love?

But we can love with
our hands combined.

O' my love,
o' my dear,
we can do it right;
your head and mine
will rise so high.

Give me your love
as I give you mine,
and love will win
the day, my
love.

Do you read me,
my love?

What do you think,
my love?

I love you so,
my heart, but say,
if you read me,
you would but
see.

Do you read me, my
love?

I think of you;
I want your love,
a day for eternity,
my dear.

Do you read me, my
love?

Do you know I love
you so?

Whisper to Me

Do I hear you say
you'll come, my dear?

My love speaks to
me again.

How can you wonder
So, my love?
Whisper to me, my love,
I plea.

How can you say you
love me so?

I can see your eyes
sparkling so, my
dear.

What makes you smile
when I come your
way?

A beauty like yours is
meant to stand;
now whisper to me,
my love.

Tell Me the Truth

Did I hear you say
your love is mine?

Did I hear you yearn
for me, my love?

Tell me, my love,
tell me the truth:
what makes you love
me so, my love?

As you can see, my
love, I say,
I yearn to know you
in and out.

Tell me the truth,
tell me, my love,
what makes you wait
the way you do?

I know you love me
all in all,
but why,
my love,
but why?

Never having a friend
is not good
for me.

Never have a friend
who laughs at your
folly and never
lets you know.

Never have a friend
who smiles
at you
but makes a fool of
you.

Never have a friend
who conspires against
you and laughs
in your face.

Should I ever have a
friend at all,
if it brings me
nothing but grief and
pain?

The rolling rock,
the rolling storm,
the tiger in haste
runs for its fray.

But I'm at home,
but I'm at sea,
counting the eggs,
but they're still
firm.

I count it once,
I count it twice,
what about the third
time, which never made
a blast?

I think it wise,
I think it best
That the bag of fault is
still alive.

My fun goes high,
my fun goes low,
but thanks to God
that I'm alive!

Preparation for an
examination is
like running a race.

The athlete picks
his challenge from the
start
and makes it all the way
through.

Getting near the tape
he gets very tired,
but he just has to
get to the end.

How would he make
it?
That is no question;
the energy in him he
uses very well.

He runs and passes the
tape so well,
how the people shout
of his victory.

But what matters most
is that
he made it up!

A Stepping Stone

Failure, as many think,
is a strong
way to doom, they
know.

But what a story she
tells me;
she is always a stepping
stone.

Many fear her sting
when she knocks
at their door.

But how many successful
individuals have never
drunk from her cup?

Kings and princes eat
from her table.

But without my failures,
I would never have
known my faults!

Familiarity and contempt
are dining together.

You go to your neighbour
too much,
you trust in him
too much,
and now he can show his
Pride.

Laughing at your problems
all through
and hiding how own
from you.

He only tells you all your
faults;
to him you're no
good.

He talks to you as if
you have a problem
in your head.

A man without a care
would die an unwanted
death.

O', See the Tears

This is the house which
Peter built;
the rat can pass,
the mouse can talk,
and Peter is strong
and good.

The house of hay,
the roof of stone,
but little Peter
cannot get in.

O', see the tears,
o', see the cry,
the mood of Peter
cannot be said.

But the mouse can
talk,
the rat can
leap;
they want to thank
Peter for a house
well built,
but Peter just sat and
wept.

The Powerful, Happy Prince

The happiest man I
know is him,
and very humble,
too.

He goes to war with
few
and comes back with many.

Wisdom rose like a
tower on a hill,
as fame goes far and
wide.

How his subject takes
to his bow!

God's love makes
him so wise,
and rich in wealth
and fame.

The best of life he
thought his own,
and never misused
his power.

His people think their
prince is wise,
for me,
for me,
I think it, too.

Like a Flowing Stream

A vegetable in a
tree
is eternity to me, I
know.

But I woke up one
morning and was
grown up.

Tell me, daylight,
tell me, dear moon,
why is it you never
change?

Your light is as
bright as ever,
and you make me forget
my days.

What would I say?

What would I do?

I see my today passing
me by.

It never cares what
I do with my life,
but just rolls and
rolls away.

I remember the day
I was young;
eternity is growing up,
but like a dream I
wake from sleep to
find my time is gone.

Why do you prove me
wrong, my day?

Like a fading dream
you are to me,
and the destiny is
already planned.

Tell me, dear light,
tell me, dear moon,
because I was young
but now I'm old,
but you seem never
to change.

In Love I Put My Hope

What should I say?

Where should I start
when my love refuses,
my love?

Ever fall in love
before, my dear?

The ocean of love
is just too deep,
and I keep sinking
down . . .
down . . .
down . . .

You never have pity
on me, my love,
and you slap my face
in the cold.

What should I say?

What should I do
when my love refuses,
my love?

I play my card,
my very best card,
for you alone, my
love.

Many call me a fool,
and maybe you do, too,
my love;
a fool maybe I am.

What would I do?

What would I say
to get your love
to me?

You know I don't
go out much,
my love,
but for you,
and you alone,
I'd come all day.

If only you knew
how much it hurts
when you stab my
heart the way you do.

Although I refuse
to cry, my love,
how you break
my heart!

How I wish I could
kiss your lips,
your eyes,
your ears . . .
a lonely man's dream,
I guess.

You are pretty, my
Love,
you are pretty,
and how I love
you so!

But when I meet
You, oh, my love,
I don't know what
to say.

How I wish I could
hold your hands
and kiss your pretty
fingers so.

How I love you,
my love,
how I love you.

And why is faith so
cruel to me,
because of the one
I love?

In love I put my hope,
I know,
and I know I will
smile again.

The Battle Is Fought and Won

Each life is a battle, I
know;
each day is a victory to
make;
each day is a history of
life,
and life is a story to
tell.

The Devil wants us to
fail,
but God is on our side.

Looking at the bright
side of the coin,
the battle is fought and
won.

Regardless of how much
I fall,
I know I will make it to
the top.

Tonight a history is made;
a good character is
unfolded;
one day I will unfold
my life and review
the history I
made.

I Remember the Day

To think of love
is what to do,
my darling one, you
hear.

A dream of love that
comes to stay;
I remember the day
my love grew
up.

She looks so bright,
she looks so nice,
as love grows up
to show the
world.

Who won't wonder
what to think,
my love,
when love glows
the way she does,
a brilliant light
within a room?

Who won't wonder
what to say, my love,
as you decide to
show yourself?

My Heart Love You

Who won't wonder
why you love me
so?

My heart yearns
so;
my heart loves
you,
a joy that comes
from joy, my love.

Thinking of you,
my love, I say,
a dream that comes
through all my
ways.

What should I say?

What should I do?

The one my heart
loves is you.

Don't Make Me Cry

My eyes are filled with
Tears, my love,
as I move
up and down the
hill.

Don't make me cry.
my love, I plea,
as I feel like sobbing
all the way through.

Can you see me?

Can you tell me
the reason why it's wet
today?

If you don't love
me, say so, my dear,
but don't make me weep
in my bed tonight.

As I move on from
bad to worse,
I wonder what to say,
my love.

Do you love me?

Do you need me?

As I move my life
from edge to edge.

What Brilliant Eyes You've Got

What a brilliant eyes you've
Got, my love;
you make me wonder
from day to day.

I love the way you look
at me;
just like a dove,
you struck at me.

I decide to make a dance;
I will dance for you,
my darling one.

You keep looking,
you keep striking;
you keep making me
love you and more.

What should I say?

What should I think,
as your eyes keep dancing
the dance of love?

I move up, dear;
I move down, love,
and I will move like
the light that struck your
eyes.

I Will Meet You

What can I say?

What can I do
to make the drum
but seems but low?

The rising sun,
the rising tide,
and more
and more;
it goes that way.

My loving one,
you have to know
that the tide of life
seems to have come.

Tell me the truth,
my loving one:
do you see truth
the way I do?

The face of life
is this, my love:
that I will meet you
in the tide of life.

The Candle Burns

The truth of life
is this, I know,
that the joy of life
is come my way.

My loving one,
my darling one,
the candle burns,
as you can
see.

Oh my, I say;
the world seems slow,
now wander on, I
must go.

My love, your eyes are
bright like stars,
and I wonder at the way
they do.

The fact of life,
what says of life,
is the truth that
mingles the way it
does.

Oh, my dear love,
oh, my dear one,
the candle is burning
so bright, my dear.

What Would I Say?

Rocking with the
rolling stone is one
thing, dear, I won't
forget.

The way you move,
the way you smile,
will rock me on and
on, my love.

Seeing the eyes that
make me smile,
seeing the joy that
brings me love,
is a laughter in moon
that makes the sky.

O mine, my dear;
oh mine, my love,
what can I say to
make you rock?

I love the move,
I love the waves;
I love the current that
you charge in me.

The Rhyming Talk

Thinking of the way you
are, my love, is
one true thing I
won't forget.

The life that mingles
day with light is the
only dream I want to
know.

My loving one,
my darling one,
the fact of life is
this, I know.

Mingling the wind with
Sky, my love,
is the love you
bring into my life,
my dear.

The rhyming talk,
the smiling lips,
the joy of life is
the words to say.

My darling one,
you have to know,
you bring me joy as
the time goes by.

The Tunnel of Life

The firing blues,
the windy air,
the joy of life as
time goes by.

Where would I go
from here, my dear,
where would I go,
my love?

I know the light of
day is bright and can
seem dull sometimes,
my love.

But in the tunnel
of life, my dear,
one thing is sure:
the spring of life still
drips, my love.

Let's smile it on;
let's smile it through,
since the joy of life
stands the test of
time.

The Bottom of Hope

How wonderful it is
to me today;
the joy of life just comes
my way.

The kiss of life,
the bright of day,
the smile that wakes
me here and now.

Wondering where to
talk of life my dear;
I know you bring my
day and life.

The truth is this, my
loving one; you wake
me up as days go
by.

You push me here;
I push you there,
as the kiss of
life breeds the hopes
we need.

Smile me through, dear,
smile me through, love;
smile me to the bottom
of hope, my love.

Your Lips but Drips

I love your smile
as it sings the song,
the song of life and
on, my dear.

I love your legs as
they swallow in the ground;
it moves with waves
that last so long.

The truth of this, my
darling one, is that you
glow with inner joy.

I know that truth
will win at last,
but the truth of it is
it moves in me.

Your eyes tell me a
loving song,
and your lips
drip with honey.

Oh, my dear one,
oh, my loved one,
the fact of life is
a story indeed.

An Arrow Shot

The water flows around
the life, and what it
says is the joy has come.

Thinking about the way you
whisper, dear,
an arrow shot,
an arrow gone.

The water flows the
way it does
and whispers love,
and then it's gone.

My darling one,
my loving one,
the gap is bridged
as life goes on.

Thinking and whispering,
days will come,
as your beautiful glow
reminds me of love.

Life will say it,
life will think it,
and life will make
the days come true.

To the lady I love, Adefolawe